HUMAN RIGHTS AT RISK

REPRODUCTIVE RIGHTS

by Tammy Gagne

BrightPoint Press

San Diego, CA

© 2025 BrightPoint Press
an imprint of ReferencePoint Press, Inc.
Printed in the United States

For more information, contact:
BrightPoint Press
PO Box 27779
San Diego, CA 92198
www.BrightPointPress.com

ALL RIGHTS RESERVED.
No part of this work covered by the copyright hereon may be reproduced or used in any form or by any means—graphic, electronic, or mechanical, including photocopying, recording, taping, web distribution, or information storage retrieval systems—without the written permission of the publisher.

LIBRARY OF CONGRESS CATALOGING-IN-PUBLICATION DATA

Names: Gagne, Tammy, author.
Title: Reproductive rights / by Tammy Gagne.
Description: San Diego, CA: BrightPoint Press, [2025] | Series: Human rights at risk | Includes bibliographical references and index. | Audience: Grades 7-9
Identifiers: LCCN 2024001078 (print) | LCCN 2024001079 (eBook) | ISBN 9781678209322 (hardcover) | ISBN 9781678209339 (eBook)
Subjects: LCSH: Reproductive rights--Juvenile literature. | Reproductive rights--History--Juvenile literature.
Classification: LCC HQ766.G26 2025 (print) | LCC HQ766 (eBook) | DDC 342.08/409--dc23/eng/20240205
LC record available at https://lccn.loc.gov/2024001078
LC eBook record available at https://lccn.loc.gov/2024001079

CONTENTS

AT A GLANCE	4
INTRODUCTION THE CASE OF SAVITA HALAPPANAVAR	6
CHAPTER ONE THE HISTORY OF REPRODUCTIVE RIGHTS	12
CHAPTER TWO ACCESS TO EDUCATION AND CONTRACEPTION	24
CHAPTER THREE ACCESS TO ABORTION	38
CHAPTER FOUR THE FUTURE OF REPRODUCTIVE RIGHTS	48
Glossary	58
Source Notes	59
For Further Research	60
Index	62
Image Credits	63
About the Author	64

AT A GLANCE

- The US federal government made birth control legal for married couples in 1965. Single women received the same right in 1972.

- The US Supreme Court case *Roe v. Wade* made abortion legal at the federal level in 1973.

- For decades, only doctors could prescribe birth control pills. But in 2016, many US states began allowing pharmacists to prescribe them as well.

- The Affordable Care Act of 2010 expanded access to birth control. It required health insurance companies to cover prescription contraception.

- In 2022, the US Supreme Court overturned *Roe v. Wade*. Women in the United States no longer had a constitutional right to abortion.

- A woman's right to an abortion is no longer guaranteed at the federal level, but some states have passed laws to guarantee that right.

- Many people disagree about whether minors have a right to keep birth control information from their parents.

- Future US elections could determine whether abortion is outlawed throughout the United States or left up to individual states.

INTRODUCTION

THE CASE OF SAVITA HALAPPANAVAR

In 2012, Savita Halappanavar was 31. She was pregnant with her first child. But 17 weeks into the pregnancy, something went wrong. Halappanavar was in intense pain. She was admitted to a hospital in Ireland. Doctors told her the **fetus** was not going to survive. She had no hope of saving her unborn child's life. Her health was also at risk. So she asked the hospital to perform an abortion. This medical

The death of Savita Halappanavar inspired activists to fight for abortion rights in Ireland.

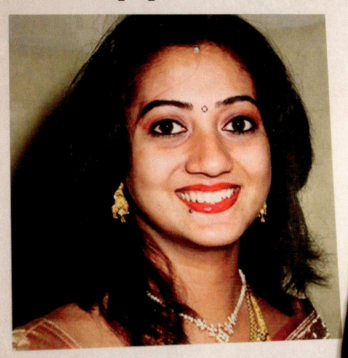

procedure ends a pregnancy. But the doctors refused to do it.

At that time, abortion was illegal in Ireland. The fetus would not live. But doctors could not perform the procedure. By law, the fetus had to die naturally.

Thousands of activists protested Ireland's law against abortion in the Annual March for Choice in September 2017.

Halappanavar waited in pain. Four days later, the fetal heartbeat stopped. Halappanavar was seriously ill. She died a few days later.

Halappanavar's death made many people speak out about abortion rights. No women in Ireland could have abortions. Not even those whose lives were in danger. **Activists** protested Ireland's strict law. They didn't want other women to die this way. Years of protests and debate followed. In 2018, Ireland held a vote about abortion. Two-thirds voted to make abortion legal.

REPRODUCTIVE RIGHTS AT RISK

Having reproductive rights means being able to decide to have children or not. It also means deciding when to have children.

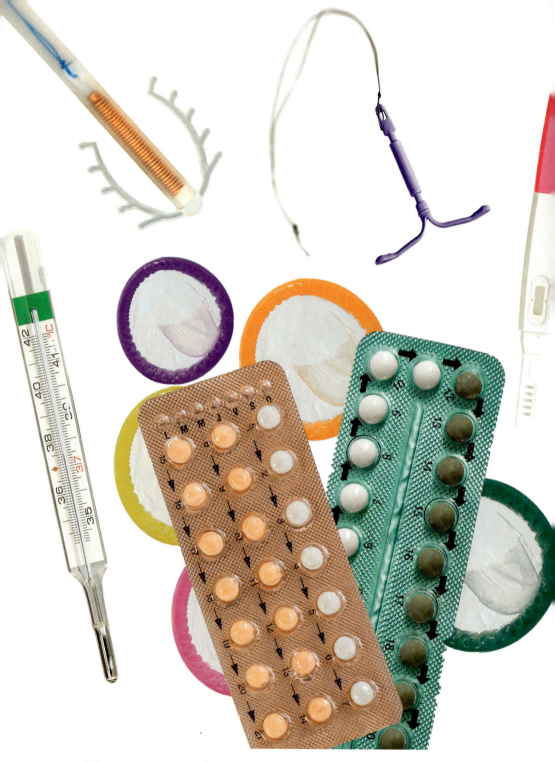

There are many different options for contraception.

Having this choice greatly affects people's lives. People may want to put off parenthood to finish school or to work. Others may not want to be parents. Access to **contraception** and abortion are key to ensuring reproductive rights.

Different factors can affect people's access to reproductive health care. One is where a person lives. That's because some governments deny the right to abortion and contraception. This is often due to religious reasons. **Poverty** can limit people's access to these rights, too. Contraception can be expensive. Reproductive rights can have a big effect on people's lives. These rights are at risk around the world.

CHAPTER ONE

THE HISTORY OF REPRODUCTIVE RIGHTS

Three American activists opened the Brownsville Clinic on October 16, 1916. They were Margaret Sanger, Ethel Byrne, and Fania Mindell. This was the first birth control clinic in the country. It was in Brooklyn, New York. The clinic gave people birth control. About 140 women showed up that first day. At this time, contraception was against the law in New York. Even sharing information about it was illegal. The state

Margaret Sanger was a key player in the founding of reproductive health clinics in the United States.

shut down the clinic nine days after it opened. All three women were arrested.

Activists kept fighting for the right to birth control. In 1923, Sanger founded two organizations. Their goal was to teach people about birth control. These groups later merged into one. It was called the Planned Parenthood Federation of America. In 1936, New York made birth control legal. Connecticut and Vermont did the same. But it would be decades before the federal government made it legal. This happened in 1965 with *Griswold v. Connecticut*. This US Supreme Court case allowed married couples to get birth control. The Supreme Court gave single women this right in 1972. This ruling was based on the case *Eisenstadt v. Baird*.

THE BIRTH CONTROL PILL

The US Food and Drug Administration (FDA) approved the first birth control pill in 1960. By 1962, 1.2 million women in the United States were using it. It became known as the pill. Access to the pill had a big effect on women's lives. It gave women more control over when or if they had children. This made it easier for women to go to college and get jobs.

Questionable Motives

In the 1930s, Margaret Sanger provided birth control to Black women in the South. Many of them lived in poverty. They could not afford to have lots of children. Sanger may have been trying to make the lives of Black people better. But some people think she was promoting **eugenics**.

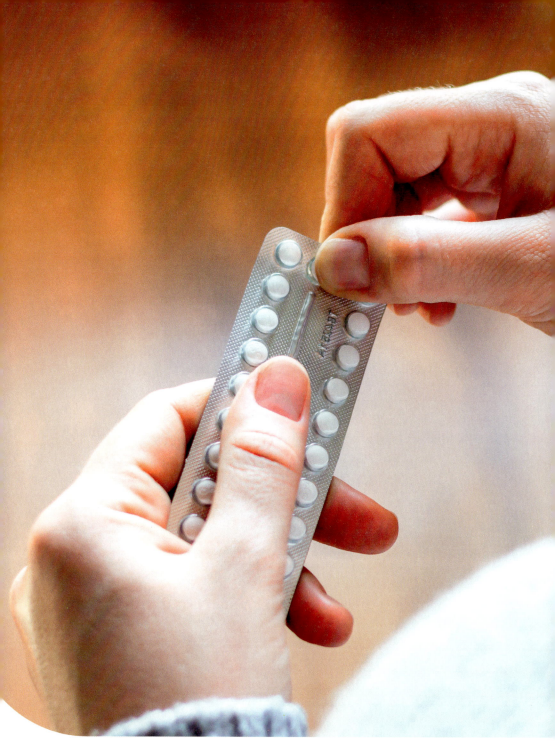

Birth control pills are one of the more popular forms of contraception.

Many women who began taking the pill still wanted children. Birth control helped them choose the right time. Pat Fishback was a young woman in the 1960s. The pill allowed her to plan her pregnancy. She could wait a couple of years after getting married to start a family. She explained this to National Public Radio (NPR) in 2020. "It also made having children a more positive experience," she said. "Because we had actually, emotionally and intellectually, gotten to the point where we really desired to have children."[1]

THE *ROE V. WADE* DECISION

In 1973, another US Supreme Court case changed reproductive rights. *Roe v. Wade* made abortion legal across the nation.

Before the case, abortion was outlawed in several states. But many women still had illegal abortions. They were not always safe. Many abortions were often done in places that were not as safe as hospitals. Sometimes the doctors used tools that had not been cleaned properly. This increased the chance of infection. Doctors didn't always know the best way to do the procedure. Many women died after unsafe abortions.

The *Roe v. Wade* decision gave reproductive rights to all women in the United States. On January 22, 1973, *CBS Evening News* anchor Walter Cronkite announced the news. He said, "In a landmark ruling, the Supreme Court today legalized abortions. . . . The decision to end

In January 1973, US Supreme Court justices voted in favor of granting reproductive rights to all women in the United States.

the pregnancy during the first three months belongs to the woman and her doctor, not the government."[2]

CHINA'S ONE-CHILD POLICY

Reproductive rights were also changing in other parts of the world. In 1979, China's population was nearing 1 billion people. The Chinese government had promoted birth control for many years. They hoped it would

For more than 30 years, many families in China could have only one child.

help slow population growth. When it did not, the government created a one-child policy. This new law was passed in 1979 but went into effect in 1980. It stated that most families could have only one child.

China insisted the policy lowered the number of births by hundreds of millions. But there were other effects. In Chinese culture, many families prefer to have sons. Sons carry on the family name. Sons also care for aging family members. A daughter joins her husband's family and cares for them instead. Families wanted sons. So many parents abandoned or killed female babies. Families did not always follow the one-child policy. These women were forced to have abortions. In 2016, China changed the law. Parents could have two children.

In 2021, the Chinese government increased the number of children families could have to three.

And in 2021, this number was increased to three. But many people still do not like the policy. Yaqiu Wang works for Human Rights Watch. She says that any limits on family size violate women's reproductive rights.

CHAPTER TWO

ACCESS TO EDUCATION AND CONTRACEPTION

Reproductive rights begin with information. Learning how women get pregnant helps people plan. They can decide if and when to have children. This helps those who want kids delay pregnancy until they are ready.

Pregnant teens are at high risk for many health problems. This includes giving birth too early. They may also have babies with low birth weights. Young people are

Finding out about a pregnancy can change a teen's life forever.

at higher risk for dying during childbirth. Women between 15 and 19 are 28 percent more likely to die during birth than women between 20 and 24.

Learning about birth control helps people avoid getting pregnant. Without this information, they may have sex without protection. This might lead to pregnancy. It also puts people at risk for sexually transmitted diseases (STDs).

Sexually Transmitted Diseases

Reproductive education often includes information about STDs. Some of these illnesses can cause death. Human papilloma virus is one of these. Others, such as chlamydia, may threaten a person's ability to have children.

Young people may have questions about their reproductive health. But they might not be comfortable talking about these issues. Classes and programs can help. A United Nations agency produced a television series. It was about the dangers of teenage pregnancy in Honduras. This Central American nation has a very high teen pregnancy rate. Watching the show helped one 12-year-old girl named Hansel Dayana Gómez. She stated, "I'm no longer afraid or ashamed to talk about sexuality and the changes I will experience."[4]

ACCESS TO BIRTH CONTROL

Birth control is widely available in many countries. But in some regions, it can still be difficult to get. About 67 percent of

Women in many African countries, including Sierra Leone, have limited access to clinics that offer contraception.

married women in high-income countries use birth control. In lower-income nations, the number is much lower. In South Sudan, only 4 percent of women use birth control. Education can affect access to birth control. Many women in developing countries do not go to school. They may not learn about reproduction. Where women live within a country makes a difference, too. Health clinics may be too far away. Women might not be able to get to a clinic.

    Birth control can even be hard to get in high-income nations. The rural United States is an example. Small clinics may not offer many birth control options. They might not have the funds, staff, or training.

    For several decades, women needed a prescription to get the birth control pill.

This is a written direction from a doctor. It allows a person to get certain medications. In 2016, many US states began to pass laws that allowed **pharmacists** to prescribe birth control pills. But many experts think the pill should be available over the counter. This means customers can buy medicine without having to ask an employee for it.

Britt Wahlin is a vice president at Ibis Reproductive Health. This organization offers reproductive services to the public. In 2019, Wahlin stated, "An over-the-counter birth control bill is long overdue in the United States. In fact, the pill is already available over the counter in more than 100 countries."[5]

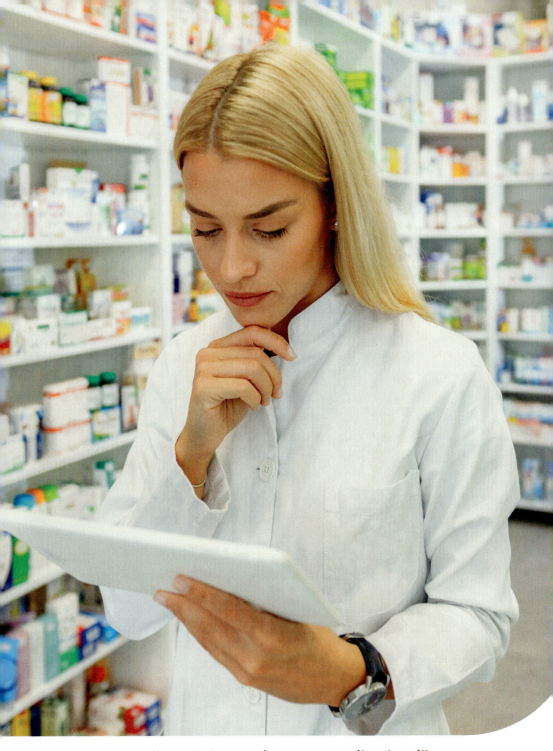

Laws that allowed pharmacists to prescribe the pill made contraception more accessible for women.

Planned Parenthood clinics offer affordable reproductive health services across the United States.

Four years later, in 2023, the FDA approved Opill. This was the first over-the-counter birth control pill. Opill was expected to be the most effective form of birth control available without a prescription.

Experts predicted that Opill would greatly expand access to birth control.

COSTS AND COVERAGE

The cost of birth control means many people can't afford it. The Affordable Care Act of 2010 helped change this. The law required health insurance companies to cover prescription birth control. This meant women would not have to pay for it. Certain insurance companies already did this. But many did not.

Many women without insurance cannot afford birth control. Planned Parenthood is one organization that helps. It offers birth control to patients without insurance. It uses a sliding scale. This means that the cost is based on a person's income. Some patients pay nothing. But government funding for these organizations was cut in the late 2010s. This meant fewer people could get birth control for free or at a lower price.

Journalist Olga Khazan wrote, "Even though birth control is now supposed to be free and easy to access, that's not always the case for poor women." Khazan explains that this is "thanks to gaps in insurance coverage, states' failure to expand **Medicaid**, and a lack of funding to a federal program that serves . . . poor women's family planning needs."[6]

THE ROLE OF RELIGION

Certain religions forbid their followers to use birth control. One of these is Catholicism. Some people who belong to these religions

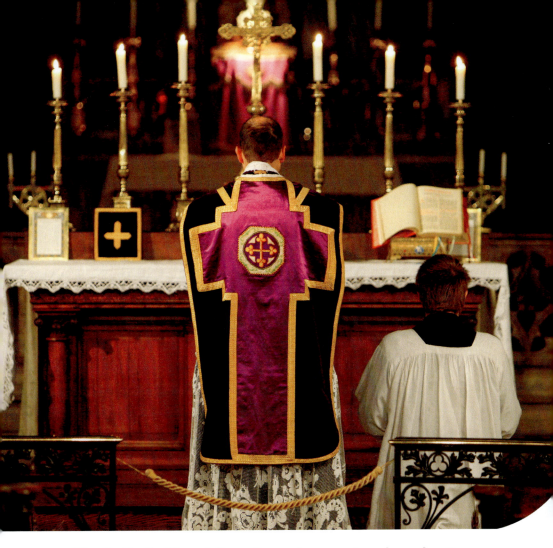

The Catholic Church has always been outspoken about its stance against contraception.

struggle with the issue. They do not want to go against their faith. But they want more control over their reproductive rights.

Religion has led some businesses to limit access to birth control. In 2020 the

Some companies have removed birth control coverage from their employee health care plans.

US Supreme Court ruled that companies could remove birth control from employee health insurance plans. Many companies did this. They were often owned by people who are against birth control for religious reasons. Like the Supreme Court, they saw the decision as a matter of religious freedom.

CHAPTER THREE

ACCESS TO ABORTION

Many people disagree about abortion. Some see abortion as a reproductive right. These people often describe themselves as pro-choice or pro-abortion rights. They think a woman should be able to choose to end a pregnancy. Others believe that abortion should be against the law. These people often call themselves pro-life or anti-abortion. They believe that life begins at **conception**.

Pro-life and pro-choice activists voice their opinions at a demonstration outside the US Supreme Court.

Some people fall somewhere in the middle. They think that abortion is acceptable in certain situations. For example, they may think a woman should be able to have an abortion when her life is at risk. Or they may be in favor of abortion in cases of rape. These differing viewpoints have led to many debates about abortion.

ABORTION AFTER *ROE V. WADE*

Abortion became more widely available after the *Roe v. Wade* decision. The ruling made it against the law for state governments to limit a woman's access to abortion. New court cases challenged the right to abortion. But for nearly five decades, the medical procedure remained legal across the nation.

People in the United States remain divided on this issue. Many states looked for ways to stop women from getting abortions. But they did it in ways that did not violate the Supreme Court's ruling. For example, some states passed laws that limited when and where women could receive the procedure. NPR journalist Deepa Shivaram reported on this issue. She said, "By 1996, 86 percent of all counties in the United

Pro-Life Violence

Some people who oppose abortion have committed violent acts. They call themselves pro-life protestors. These people have attacked women seeking abortions. They have also committed violent crimes against abortion providers.

States did not have a known abortion provider."[7] This meant that a woman who wanted an abortion could not get one without traveling far away. And some of the women could not afford to do that.

ROE V. WADE, OVERTURNED

Abortion became one of the biggest issues of the 2016 US presidential election. Hillary Clinton ran against Donald Trump. Abortion came up often in the campaign. During one of the debates, Clinton made a promise to the audience. "I will defend *Roe v. Wade*. I will defend a woman's right to make her own decision," she said.[8]

Trump disagreed. He stated that he was anti-abortion. If he became the president, he said he would appoint Supreme Court

Many who supported Hillary Clinton during the 2016 presidential campaign voted for her because she was pro abortion rights.

justices who would overturn *Roe v. Wade.* He thought each state should be able to decide whether abortion is legal. As president, he followed through with this campaign promise.

President Trump appointed three justices to the US Supreme Court. They were Neil Gorsuch, Brett Kavanaugh, and Amy Coney Barrett. Trump lost the 2020 election to Joe Biden. But Supreme Court justices can remain in power for life. Although they may retire, few have done so.

On June 24, 2022, the US Supreme Court ruled on a case. *Dobbs v. Jackson Women's Health Organization* involved a law in Mississippi that banned abortions at 15 weeks of pregnancy. The court's ruling overturned *Roe v. Wade*. As a result, women's constitutional right to abortion was gone.

In the months that followed, eighteen states passed new laws on abortion. Some severely restricted the procedure. Others banned it in nearly all circumstances. Many states also began working on laws to change access to abortion.

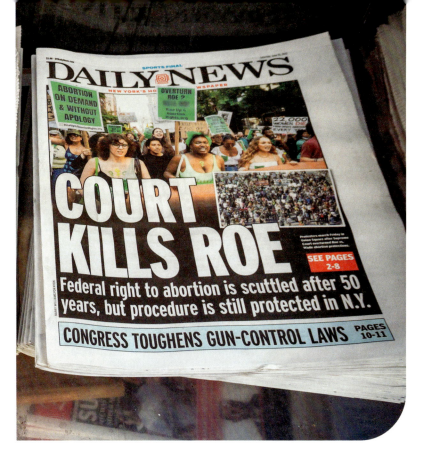

After 50 years, a woman's right to an abortion was overturned by the US Supreme Court in 2022.

NEW ABORTION LAWS

In 2023, South Carolina and Florida passed abortion laws. Each state banned abortion in most cases after the sixth week of pregnancy. Both laws make exceptions in cases of rape or **incest**. They also allow an abortion if the woman's life is at risk.

STATES WITH ABORTION BANS

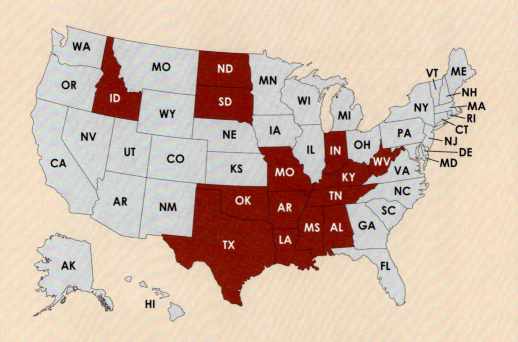

Source: Annette Choi and Devan Cole. "See Where Abortions Are Banned and Legal—and Where It's in Limbo." *CNN*, November 7, 2023. www.cnn.com.

The states shown in red had a ban on abortion in most cases in 2023.

Abortion is allowed if the fetus has a fatal condition. But in these states it is very difficult to get approval for one of these exceptions. Or approval isn't granted in time for the abortion to be performed safely.

Some people are against these laws. They point out that many women do not know they are pregnant until after the sixth week. Women seeking an abortion in these states may have to wait for an appointment. By the time they can see a doctor, they may be more than 6 weeks pregnant. That would make the procedure illegal.

Some states have also outlawed medications called abortion pills. These pills end a pregnancy without surgery. In 2020, more than half the abortions in the United States involved abortion pills. In 2023, several court cases were filed against the FDA that could outlaw the medications. This would make the pills illegal even in states where abortion is legal.

CHAPTER FOUR

THE FUTURE OF REPRODUCTIVE RIGHTS

Reproductive rights will likely be challenged in the future. Many experts think that some groups opposed to abortion will try to outlaw birth control. Lawmakers have taken steps to prevent this from happening. In 2023, Democrats in Congress introduced a bill that would protect people's rights to birth control.

There were some Republicans who insisted that the Democrats were trying to

The fate of reproductive rights often depends on who wins the next election.

scare the American people with the move. Representative Kat Cammack stated, "This bill is completely unnecessary. In no way, shape, or form is access to contraception limited or at risk of being limited."[10]

But some forms of birth control were already being targeted. In 2021, Idaho banned state-funded student health centers from offering emergency contraception. These medications prevent pregnancy after sexual intercourse.

Students do still have access to standard birth control methods at student health centers. These centers are not funded by the state. This means the state of Idaho cannot impose the ban on birth control at these sites. Those who work at these centers are not university employees.

Providing minors with confidential access to birth control can reduce the number of teen pregnancies.

MINORS' ACCESS TO BIRTH CONTROL

Young people are at risk of losing access to birth control. In December 2020, a federal judge in Texas ruled against young people's rights to privacy about birth control.

The case *Deanda v. Becerra* questioned whether minors had a right to keep birth control information from their parents. The judge ruled that a family planning program violated parents' rights by keeping minors' use of the program private.

People who agree with this ruling think that parents have a right to know if their children seek birth control services. But one in five people between 15 and 17 say they would not use such a program if their parents would be told. Programs that provide birth control to minors help reduce teen risks for pregnancy and STDs. Without family planning services, these risks are much higher. Clare Coleman is CEO of the National Family Planning and Reproductive Health Association. She explains that if

Norgestrel was approved in 2023 and was first available under the name Opill in 2024.

teens can't privately receive care, they won't seek health services.

Minors can get some forms of birth control without seeing a doctor. This includes condoms. They are available at most drug stores. In 2023, Dr. Mary A. Ott and Dr. Elizabeth M. Alderman wrote about the FDA's approval of norgestrel. They stated, "There will be no minimum age limit . . . adolescents will be allowed to purchase the new over-the-counter pill."[12] But people may need to pay for this form of birth control themselves. Often the cost isn't covered by insurance.

State insurance laws may also make it harder for minors to get the birth control pill without a prescription. In some states, minors can ask insurance companies for privacy. In certain situations, this is true even when they are covered by their parent's policies. But in other states, privacy laws prevent the companies from honoring this request.

STATE OR FEDERAL LAW?

Abortion has long been a key issue in US elections. This was especially true after the 2022 ruling in *Dobbs v. Jackson Women's*

Many Americans believe reproductive rights, including the right to an abortion, are key human rights.

Health Organization. However, polling has shown that most Americans actually agree about abortion rights. For example, a

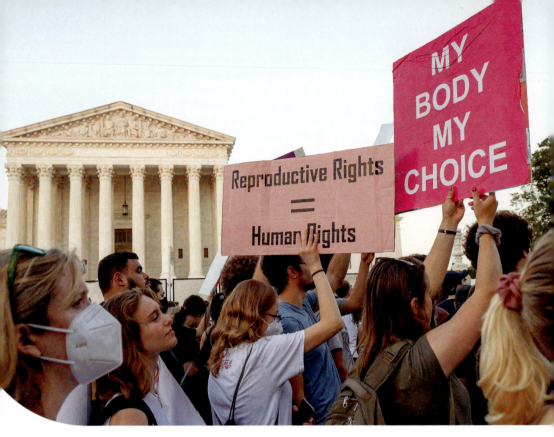

The majority of Americans agree that abortion should be legal in most instances.

2023 poll by the Associated Press and the National Opinion Research Center found that 64 percent of Americans said abortion should be legal in all or most cases.

Several groups work to make sure everyone has access to birth control. These include the American Civil Liberties Union, the Center for Reproductive Rights, and Planned Parenthood. These groups also aim to make birth control available around the world. But their work depends on future court rulings and elections in the United States and elsewhere.

Adoption Is a Reproductive Right

Reproductive rights include access to adoption. But adoption can be difficult for some. Members of the **LGBTQ** community are often overlooked for adoption. Gay couples are allowed to adopt in all US states. But thirteen states allow state-licensed adoption agencies to deny adoptions for religious reasons. This means heterosexual couples are often given preference.

GLOSSARY

activists

people who gather to speak out about controversial issues

conception

the process of becoming pregnant

contraception

devices or medications that prevent pregnancy

eugenics

the practice of selective breeding among humans to control genetic composition

fetus

an offspring of a human or other mammal in the stages of prenatal development

incest

sexual relations between people who are related

LGBTQ

Lesbian, gay, bisexual, transgender, and queer

Medicaid

a government program designed to help people afford medical care

pharmacists

people licensed to dispense medication

SOURCE NOTES

CHAPTER ONE: THE HISTORY OF REPRODUCTIVE RIGHTS

1. Quoted in Sarah McCammon, "How the Approval of the Birth Control Pill 60 Years Ago Helped Change Lives," *NPR News*, May 9, 2020. www.npr.org.

2. Quoted in Jonathan Miller, "How CBS News Covered *Roe v. Wade* in 1973," *CBS News*, January 22, 2023. www.cbsnews.com.

CHAPTER TWO: ACCESS TO EDUCATION AND CONTRACEPTION

3. Quoted in "Education Is a Reproductive Health Issue," *USA for UNFPA*, n.d. www.usaforunfpa.org.

4. Quoted in Sian Ferguson, "A Teen's Guide to the Best Birth Control Methods," *Healthline*, May 26, 2021. www.healthline.com.

5. Quoted in Olga Khazan, "Why Some Women Still Can't Get Birth Control," *The Atlantic*, November 2, 2016. www.theatlantic.com.

CHAPTER THREE: ACCESS TO ABORTION

6. Quoted in Deepa Shivaram, "The Movement Against Abortion Rights Is Nearing Its Apex," *NPR News*, May 4, 2022. www.npr.org.

7. Quoted in Dan Mangan, "Trump: I'll Appoint Supreme Court Justices to Overturn *Roe v. Wade* Abortion Case," *CNBC News*, October 19, 2016. www.cnbc.com.

CHAPTER FOUR: THE FUTURE OF REPRODUCTIVE RIGHTS

8. Quoted in Christina Cauterucci, "Birth Control Is Next," *Slate*, April 21, 2023. www.slate.com.

9. Quoted in Mary A. Ott and Elizabeth Alderman, "Contraception Explained," *Healthy Children.org*, n.d. www.healthychildren.org.

FOR FURTHER RESEARCH

BOOKS

Tammy Gagne, *Refugee and Immigrant Rights*. San Diego, CA: BrightPoint Press, 2024.

Jennifer Lombardo, *The Story of the Women's Suffrage Movement*. Buffalo, NY: Cavendish Square, 2024.

Philip Wolny, *Gender Violence*. San Diego, CA: BrightPoint Press, 2025.

INTERNET SOURCES

"Reproductive Rights Are LGBTQ+ Rights," *Human Rights Campaign*, Spring 2022. www.hrc.org.

"Reproductive Rights in America," *NPR*, n.d. www.npr.org.

"*Roe v. Wade* and Supreme Court Abortion Cases," *Brennan Center for Justice*, September 28, 2022. www.brennancenter.org.

WEBSITES

American Civil Liberties Union (ACLU)
www.aclu.org

The ACLU defends and preserves individual rights as guaranteed by the US Constitution.

Center for Reproductive Rights
www.reproductiverights.org

The Center for Reproductive Rights ensures that reproductive rights are protected as fundamental human rights.

Planned Parenthood
www.plannedparenthood.org

Planned Parenthood provides family planning services to people regardless of their ability to pay.

INDEX

abortion laws, 45–47, 56
adoption, 57
Affordable Care Act, 33

Barrett, Amy Coney, 44
birth control pill, 15, 16, 29–30, 32, 54
Brownsville Clinic, 12
Byrne, Ethel, 12

Cammack, Kat, 50
Clinton, Hillary, 42
contraception, 10, 11, 12, 24, 35, 38, 50
Cronkite, Walter, 18

Deanda v. Becerra, 52
Dobbs v. Jackson Women's Health Organization, 44, 54

Eisenstadt v. Baird, 14
eugenics, 15

Fishback, Pat, 17
Food and Drug Administration (FDA), 15, 32, 47, 53

Gorsuch, Neil, 43
Griswold v. Connecticut, 14

Halappanavar, Savita, 6–9

Ibis Reproductive Health, 30

Kavanaugh, Brett, 43

LGBTQ, 57

Medicaid, 34
Mindell, Fania, 12

norgestrel, 32, 53

one-child policy, 20–23

Planned Parenthood, 14, 33, 57
pro-choice, 38, 43
pro-life, 38, 41, 42

religion, 34–35, 37
Roe v. Wade, 17–18, 40, 42–44

Sanger, Margaret, 12, 14, 15
sexually transmitted diseases (STDs), 26, 52

Trump, Donald, 42–44

IMAGE CREDITS

Cover: © Jim West/Alamy Live News/Alamy
5: © Kevin Dietsch/UPI/Alamy
7: © TC/Alamy
8: © Briley/Shutterstock Images
10: © JPC-PROD/Shutterstock Images
13: © Alpha Historica/Alamy
16: © itakdalee/Shutterstock Images
19: © Gary Blakeley/Shutterstock Images
20: © TonyV3112/Shutterstock Images
22: © TonyV3112/Shutterstock Images
25: © Marcos Mesa Sam Wordley/Shutterstock Images
28: © Jonathan Porter/Alamy
31: © Aleksandar Karanov/Shutterstock Images
32: © Ken Wolter/Shutterstock Images
35: © godongphoto/Shutterstock Images
36: © SatawatK/Shutterstock Images
39: © Jeff McCoy/Shutterstock Images
43: © Joseph Sohm/Shutterstock Images
45: © rblfmr/Shutterstock Images
46: © Red Line Editorial
49: © f11photo/Shutterstock Images
51: © Antonio Guillem/Shutterstock Images
53: © luchschenF/Shutterstock Images
55: © Lyonstock/Shutterstock Images
56: © Ben Von Klemperer/Shutterstock Images

ABOUT THE AUTHOR

Tammy Gagne is a freelance writer and editor who specializes in educational nonfiction for young people. She has written hundreds of books on a wide range of topics. Some of her favorite projects have been about women's issues. Gagne resides in northern New England with her husband, son, and dogs.